D0401228

WELCOME TO
PASSPORT TO READING
A beginning reader's ticket to a brand-new world!

Every book in this program is designed to build read-along and read-alone skills, level by level, through engaging and enriching stories. As the reader turns each page, he or she will become more confident with new vocabulary, sight words, and comprehension.

These PASSPORT TO READING levels will help you choose the perfect book for every reader.

READING TOGETHER
Read short words in simple sentence structures together to begin a reader's journey.

READING OUT LOUD
Encourage developing readers to sound out words in more complex stories with simple vocabulary.

READING INDEPENDENTLY
Newly independent readers gain confidence reading more complex sentences with higher word counts.

READY TO READ MORE
Readers prepare for chapter books with fewer illustrations and longer paragraphs.

This book features sight words from the educator-supported Dolch Sight Words List. This encourages the reader to recognize commonly used vocabulary words, increasing reading speed and fluency.

For more information, please visit passporttoreadingbooks.com.

Enjoy the journey!

Little, Brown and Company

Hachette Book Group
1290 Avenue of the Americas, New York, NY 10104
Visit us at lb-kids.com

Little, Brown and Company is a division of Hachette Book Group, Inc.
The Little, Brown name and logo are trademarks of Hachette Book Group, Inc.
The publisher is not responsible for websites (or their content)
that are not owned by the publisher.

First Edition: December 2016

Library of Congress Control Number: 2016946552

ISBN 978-0-316-39377-5

10 9 8 7 6 5 4 3 2

CW

Printed in the United States of America

Passport to Reading titles are leveled by independent reviewers applying the standards
developed by Irene Fountas and Gay Su Pinnell in *Matching Books to Readers:
Using Leveled Books in Guided Reading*, Heinemann, 1999.

Licensed By:

TRANSFORMERS RESCUE BOTS
TRAINING ACADEMY

DINOSAURS!

by Trey King

LITTLE, BROWN AND COMPANY
New York   Boston

Cody needs a new subject for the next
Training Academy manual.
"Do you have any ideas?" Cody asks.
"I do," Optimus Prime says.
"Let us teach the Rescue Bots
about **dinosaurs**.
It is one of their other modes."

"That is a great idea," Cody says.
"But dinosaurs are not alive anymore.
Where can I learn about them?"
Optimus Prime says,
"The Griffin Rock Natural History
Museum, of course!"

The word "dinosaur" comes from the
Greek words meaning "terrible lizard."
Some thought the name came
from dinosaurs' teeth and claws.
It actually came from their huge size.

Wow.
They are huge!

FUN FACT

Dinosaurs died a long time ago. That means dinosaurs and humans never lived together at the same time.
That is good for us! Some dinosaurs would want to eat us!

The **Tyrannosaurus rex** is probably
the most well-known dinosaur.
It was large and very hungry.

FUN FACT

"Rex" means "king" in Latin.

A T. rex could weigh up to 18,000 pounds—
that is about the same as 100 people!
One tooth found was almost
12 inches long!

The **stegosaurus** was another large dinosaur.

It was a plant eater.

It had rows of plates on its back and spikes on its tail.

FUN FACT

Although its body was rather large, a stegosaurus's brain was small—around the same size as a lime.

I would not want to mess with that dinosaur!

Do not worry. They were rather slow. Their maximum speed is believed to be about five miles per hour.

The **apatosaurus** and **brontosaurus** were similar in size.
Some scientists think they are the same dinosaur. Others do not.

FUN FACT

Apatosaurus was an **herbivore**—meaning it only ate plants.

These dinosaurs are some of the largest animals to have ever walked the Earth. They were about 75 feet long— that's about as long as two school buses.

FUN FACT

Heatwave's dino mode is a brachiosaurus. It was very similar to apatosaurus in shape, but was much bigger.

The **triceratops** had three horns and
a large bone frill around its neck.

These helped

protect it from

the T. rex.

FUN FACT

Humans have 32 teeth in their mouths. The triceratops had up to 800 teeth!

15

Velociraptors were smaller than humans—about the height of a turkey! It is believed that they had feathers!

The velociraptor is thought to have used the curved claws on its feet to get food.

Where are its manners? Could you imagine if I ate with my feet?

FUN FACT

The NBA basketball team based in Toronto, Canada, named themselves the Toronto Raptors after the famous dinosaur.

There were lots of different types of **pterodactyls**.

Some were as small as crows.

Others were as big as hang gliders!

The term "dinosaur" refers to animals that WALKED on land. But pterodactyls could fly. That means they are NOT dinosaurs!

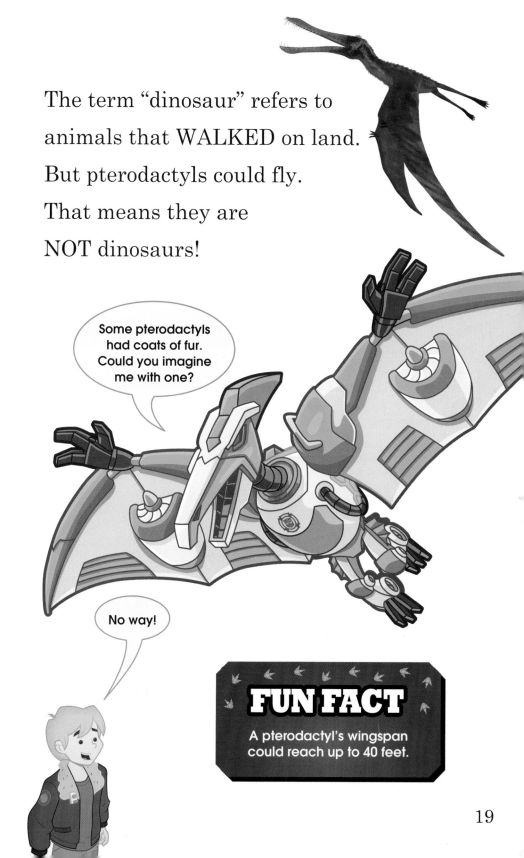

Some pterodactyls had coats of fur. Could you imagine me with one?

No way!

FUN FACT

A pterodactyl's wingspan could reach up to 40 feet.

Dinosaurs roamed on land.

Other reptiles stayed in the water.

The **shastasaurus** is one of the largest
marine reptile species ever found.
But it was not a fearsome predator—
it ate mostly fish and squid.

Recognize the **archelon**?
This giant turtle could live up to
100 years.

The **sarcosuchus** was a relative
of the crocodile.
Though it was twice as big, it still liked
to swim in rivers and wait for dinner.

The **tanystropheus** lived
in shallow water.
Sometimes it came onto land
to eat insects.

Perhaps I should use
one of these for my dino
mode! Which one would
YOU choose?

No one knows for sure how many kinds of dinosaurs existed.

So far, between 250 and 550 have been found.

iguanodon

dimetrodon

ankylosaurus

23

Dinosaurs came in all shapes and sizes.
The smallest—the **compsognathus**—
was barely larger than a chicken.
It weighed about 12 pounds.

One of the largest dinosaurs—
the **argentinosaurus**—was found
by a rancher in Argentina.

I knew dinosaurs were big, but I didn't know they could be so small!

Humans came long after dinosaurs.
But **fossils** have helped us figure out a lot
of what we know—like how dinosaurs
acted and what they may have looked like.

Because dinosaur bones are
old and fragile, big diggers and trucks
cannot dig them out.
They must be carved out of the ground
slowly by people with tiny tools.

Once bones are taken out of the ground,
they are packed very carefully.
Each bone gets its own box.
Then, the bones are taken to museums all
over the world for people to see and study.

Sometimes they are taken by truck. Sometimes they are taken by helicopter!

That is where I come in!

"That was amazing!" Cody says.

"There is so much to learn about dinosaurs—
and about the rest of the world, too!
I cannot wait to start my next training manual."

Anything with animals gets my vote!

Go back and read this story again—
but this time, see if you can **sound out**
all the dinosaurs' names!

Tyrannosaurus rex
(ti-**ran**-uh-**sawr**-us reks)

triceratops
(try-**ser**-uh-**tops**)

apatosaurus
(ah-**pa**-tuh-**sawr**-us)

velociraptor
(veh-la-sih-**rap**-tor)

brontosaurus
(**bron**-tuh-**sawr**-us)

pterodactyl
(**ter**-uh-**dak**-til)

stegosaurus
(**steg**-uh-**sawr**-us)

ankylosaurus
(**ank**-eh-lo-**sawr**-us)